Oakl., Califf. Freemasons Live Oak Lodge No. 61

Souvenir. Fortieth Anniversary Live Oak Lodge no. 61

A.M., Oakland, Cal. Instituted Friday evening, August 19, 1854.

Anniversary exercises, held Friday evening, August 17, 1894, including

history of lodge and roll of members

Oakl., Califf. Freemasons Live Oak Lodge No. 61

Souvenir. Fortieth Anniversary Live Oak Lodge no. 61
A.M., Oakland, Cal. Instituted Friday evening, August 19, 1854. Anniversary exercises, held Friday evening, August 17, 1894, including history of lodge and roll of members

ISBN/EAN: 9783337268206

Printed in Europe, USA, Canada, Australia, Japan

Cover: Foto ©Andreas Hilbeck / pixelio.de

More available books at **www.hansebooks.com**

MASONIC TEMPLE.
Home of Live Oak Lodge, No. 61.
Dedicated Feb. 22, 1871.

SOUVENIR

FORTIETH ANNIVERSARY

LIVE OAK LODGE

No. 61, F. & A. M.

OAKLAND, CAL.

Instituted Friday Evening, August 19, 1854

Anniversary Exercises, held Friday Evening, August 17, 1894

—— INCLUDING ——

History of Lodge and Roll of Members.

Brazen Pillars,
Hall of Live Oak Lodge.

FORTIETH ANNIVERSARY

_{OF}

LIVE OAK LODGE, NO. 61, F. and A. M.

_{OF}

OAKLAND, CALIFORNIA.

HELD AT

MASONIC TEMPLE, AUGUST 17, 1894.

At stated meeting of June 1, 1894, the following resolution was unanimously adopted:—

WHEREAS, Live Oak Lodge, No. 61, F. and A. M., was organized August 19, 1854, thereby becoming the pioneer of Masonry in Alameda County, and

WHEREAS, we find ample cause for gratitude that under the guidance of the Supreme Grand Master, we are enjoying an era of prosperity and perfect harmony, within our own portals, and with the fraternity in general, therefore be it

Resolved, that the Worshipful Master be and is hereby authorized to appoint a committee of five, in addition to himself (he to act as ex-officio chairman), with power to formulate a program and make all necessary arrangements for an evening's entertainment some time in August, which will be a fitting celebration of so important an event in the history of Live Oak Lodge as the Fortieth Anniversary of its Organization.

In conformity with the above resolution the Master appointed the following: The Senior Warden, John A.

4

Beckwith; the Secretary. J. J. Warner; Past Masters, Harry C. Bush and A. W. Bishop; Musical Director, George H. Carleton.

Charles E. Haven, W. M., Chairman.

The committee arranged the following program:—

LIVE OAK LODGE. NO. 61, F. & A. M.

1854—OAKLAND, AUG. 17—1894.

FORTIETH ANNIVERSARY.

PROGRAM

Quartet, "Annie Laurie" - - - *D. Buck*

Masonic Quartet

Prayer, - - - - - - -

Rev. Alfred T. Perkins, Grand Chaplain

Greeting, - - - - - - -

J. C. Martin, P. M.

"Welcome, welcome do I sing,
Far more welcome than the Spring."

Song, "Flight of Ages" - - - - *Bevan*

Mrs. Olive Reed Batchelder

Chronicle, - - - - - - -

A. W. Bishop, P. M.

"The bell strikes one; we take no note of time
but from its loss.
To give it then a tongue is wise in man."

Song, "Rose Marie" - - - - - *Molloy*

Ben Clark

Address, "Masonry—Its Cardinal Virtues" -

Brother D. L. Smoot

"Here wisdom calls, 'Seek virtue first, be bold;
As gold to silver, virtue is to gold.' "

Song, "For all Eternity" *Mascheroni*

Mrs. Martin Schultz

French horn solo (selected) -

Joseph Reiter, late soloist of Vienna Prater Orchestra

Address, "The Grand Lodge of Masons of California"

M. M. Estee, P. G. M.

"For we are the same that our fathers have been:
We see the same lights that our fathers have seen;
We drink the same stream, we view the same sun,
And run the same course that our fathers have run."

Song, "The Gallant Vaquero" - - *M. Watson*

H. H. Lawrence, Jr.

Intermission—Ten-minutes' social

Song, "Snow" - - - - - - *Parker*

Mrs. Martin Schultz

Address, - - - - -

Brother H. C. McPike

"Lady," he cried, "I have sworn to-night
On the word of a fairy knight
To do my sentence task aright."

Duet, "The Moon Has Raised Her Lamp above -

- - - - - - - *Jules Benedict*

Ben Clark and H. H. Lawrence, Jr.

Goodnight, - - - - -

J. R. Glascock, P. M.

"Whene'er we grasp the hand of those
We would be forever nigh,
The flame of friendship bursts and glows
In warm, frank words, 'Goodbye!'"

CHARLES EDWARD HAVEN.
Born in San Jose, Cal., Aug. 7, 1861.
M. M. Live Oak Lodge, Dec. 10, 1886.
The Present Master, 1894.

Quartet (selected), -   -   -   -   -   -

Masonic Quartet

Benediction, -   -   -   -   -   -   -   -

Rev. Benj. Akerly, P. M.

Masonic Quartet: Ben Clark, H. M. Baker, H. H. Lawrence,
Jr., George H. Carleton. Accompanists: Brother
H. O. Hunt, Martin Schultz, and Louis Homeier.

The Lodge was opened at 7:30 P. M. on the third
degree, and then adjourned to the large hall on the second
floor of the temple, which was tastefully decorated with a
representation of a live oak tree back of the stage, draped
with the stars and stripes, the stage being surrounded by
a variety of foliage.

When the hour for the opening of the exercises had
arrived (eight o'clock), the hall was completely filled by
the Masonic fraternity, their families, and friends.
Among the distinguished members of the fraternity present were: M. W. Morris March Estee, Past Grand Master;
R. W. James Baunty Stevens, Deputy Grand Master; V. W. George Johnson, Grand Secretary; W.
Elias C. Hare, Grand Lecturer; Brother Edwin A Sherman, National President, Masonic Veteran Association of
the United States, and Secretary of the Masonic Veteran
Association of the Pacific Coast; Ebenezer Winchester,
Past Master of American Union Lodge, No 1, Marietta,
Ohio. The Worshipful Master, Charles E. Haven, presided, and, on calling the assemblage to order, he stated
that seats had been provided near the stage for all present
who had been Master Masons forty years or more, and
invited all such to come forward and occupy them. The
following brethren responded to the invitation:—

Edwin A. Sherman.
Ebenezer Winchester.
Franklin Warner.
Orville K. Stampley.
Richard Cassidy.
Andrew J. Snyder.
Charles B. Rutherford.
Joseph R. Kendall.
Reynolds Landon.

The Worshipful Master then announced the object of the meeting in a few well-chosen words, when the Masonic Quartet sang the first number on the program, "Annie Laurie," Brother H O Hunt, organist of Live Oak Lodge, playing the piano accompaniment. Then followed an eloquent invocation to the Great Architect of the Universe for his blessing upon the Lodge and its members, and the craft in general, by Rev. Alfred T. Perkins, Grand Chaplain of the Grand Lodge of California.

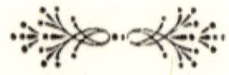

The Greeting.

The "Greeting" address was then delivered by Brother James C. Martin, P. M., as follows: —

It is a pleasant duty on this the fortieth anniversary of Live Oak Lodge to salute all here with words of greeting and of welcome.

Forty years is a long span in human life. All who may now be considered young were unborn when Live Oak Lodge was started upon its mission. Those who were infants then are now passing the meridian of life. Those who were then young are now growing old, and all who were then old are dead.

But how short is this span in the life of Freemasonry; its authentic history runs back more than three thousand years. During its existence a procession of more than one hundred and fifty generations of mankind have successively arisen and have successively passed on into eternity. But its lights are not dimmed, its supports are not weakened, and its beauties are not faded. It was never brighter, it was never stronger, its teachings and its truths were never fresher, than now.

There have been times in the world's history when almost all the germs of human progress were guarded, fortified, and nourished by Freemasonry.

There are places in the world where almost all that tends to make men better and nobler is clustered about its altars.

There is no country in which its lodges do not exist; there is no language in which its ritual is not spoken; and

JAMES CHRISTOPHER MARTIN.

Born in Morgan County, Illinois, Nov. 14, 1839.
M. M. Chico Lodge, No. 111, Chico, Cal., 1865.
Was W. M. in 1875-1880-81.

always and everywhere it has been the friend and advo-
cate of advancement, of learning, of literature, of the arts
and sciences, of order, of law and of liberty.

It has never made war upon organized society or upon
established governments. It as never assailed an honestly
entertained religious belief or creed.

It addresses itself to individual conscience and individual intelligence and thus reaches the utmost limits of the
circle in which the individual moves.

The time may come when its light will be extinguished,
its altars abandoned and its temples deserted, but that can
only be when the passions and prejudices of men shall
need no restraint, when there shall be no imposition or
oppression; when there shall be no distress; when the mil-
lennium shall fully come.

Every lodge in the world is devoted to the same end and
purpose with all other lodges and is especially entitled to
consideration with all others.

But it is but natural that the members of Live Oak
Lodge should feel special pride in its history, and it was a
happy and loyal expression that suggested this association
to commemorate the fortieth anniversary of its establish-
ment.

By our presence here we express our high esteem for
its founders and for all who have preceded us in faithful
membership, we pay merited tribute to the memory of
our honored dead, and we are enabled to exchange with
the living mutual encouragement and congratulations.

And while bespeaking some indulgence for fervid expression of pardonable pride on the part of its members,
Live Oak Lodge, with such entertainment as it may offer,
greets each individual, anointed friend or brother, in
hearty Saxon, with good hail and welcome.

AMASA WRIGHT BISHOP,
Historian
Born in Wallingford, Vermont. Aug. 18, 1832.
M. M. White Rock Lodge, U. D., 1858.
Was W. M. Vesper Lodge, No. 84, 1863 4 5.
Member Live Oak Lodge since 1876.

Forty Years Ago.

HISTORICAL SKETCH OF THE LODGE.

BY AMASA WRIGHT BISHOP, P. M.,

HISTORIAN.

BRETHREN AND FRIENDS: The pleasant duty assigned me this anniversary evening is that of presenting to you a historical sketch of Live Oak Lodge, embracing a period of forty years, from the date of its institution to the present. The greatest difficulty which I have encountered in the preparation of this sketch, is that of condensation to limits that would not tire your patience, and still be satisfactory as a history of the lodge.

As I delved in the musty records of the past and dug from their graves the ghosts of departed years, resurrecting the names of the old brotherhood, the thought came over me, how few the number of those present would recognize the pioneer brethren of our sodality, fraters of a past generation.

There are three important periods in the life of man, each distinct from the others.

First: Boyhood or youth, the years of which are lived in the aspirations and hopes of the gilded future. And the days and months and years of this period are all too slow that keeps ardent youth from the enjoyment of the highly wrought pictures of that future.

The second is that of mature manhood, the period when

man lives in the present; when all of his energies are devoted to the present; and the years are less roseate than the youth's dream of the future; for he has learned that "life is real, life is earnest;" that life has its shadows and shades as well as its sunshine; its disappointments as well as its successes; he has learned patience—learned to labor and to wait.

The third period is that of age, when man lives mostly in the past. The farther he descends the western declivity of the hill of life toward the sunset, and as he approaches the period when life's shadows are meeting eternity's day, and the gates of the sunset are opening for admittance to the night which precedes the morn of eternal life, the more he lives in the past. And while memory may fail to retain the impressions of the few preceding years, or even months, the panorama of his early life becomes more vivid, and the incidents of early days stand out in bold relief, as if they had transpired only in the yesterdays just past.

This evening I shall be able to present only a skeleton panorama of the past forty years, leaving to you, my hearers, the pleasing duty of filling in the woof that shall make the perfect web—the shadings that shall make the perfect picture.

Let your imagination go back to the Oakland of forty years ago—to the little hamlet of a few hundred people—and compare it with the magnificent city, the Oakland of to-day, with its 60,000 people, and as you follow the history of Live Oak Lodge, let your imagination note the wonderful changes in this city, as well as those of the lodge, as the years pass in review. Contrast the primitive lodge room over a stable on the water front with this magnificent temple, and the Masonic band of a score of

Masons with the thousand or more which now swell the ranks of the fraternity of this city. The Grand Master of Masons of California granted a dispensation to certain brethren of Oakland to open a lodge of Master Masons, and to initiate, pass and raise all good men and true who might apply, they finding them worthy.

On Friday evening, August 19, 1854, just forty years ago this Friday night, these brethren met in a building owned by Edson Adams, at the foot of Broadway, near the wharf, the then business center of the embryo city, and organized Live Oak Lodge, the following brethren acting as officers: Lawrence C. Owen, Worshipful Master; Isaac E. Paddock, Senior Warden; Jeremiah E. Whitcher, Junior Warden; and Samuel H. Robinson, Secretary.

Of these officers not one remains on earth to-day. All have responded to the call of the Supreme Grand Master of the universe—"Come up hither!"—and they have taken their stations in the Celestial Lodge above, according to their true merits, tried by the square of virtue and morality.

Brother Lawrence C. Owen, the Master, for many years filled the office of Assistant Grand Secretary, also Secretary of the Grand Chapter and Recorder of the Grand Commandery. The last years of his life were years of misfortune and reason dethroned.

Brother Isaac E. Paddock, the Senior Warden, was elected the first Master of the lodge under its charter. After serving his term he left Oakland for the southern part of the State, where he engaged in business, and where he died a few years thereafter.

Brother Jeremiah E. Whitcher, the Junior Warden, was elected Master of the lodge in 1859, and again in 1860. He was city engineer during the years of 1854-55-56,

LAWERANCE CONLEY OWEN.
Born in New York State, 1827.
M. M. Geo. Washington Lodge, No. 65, New Orleans, 1852.
Petitioner for Dispensation and Charter Member.
Was Master under Dispensation, 1854
Died Dec. 21, 1874.

laid out and made an official map of a large portion of the city. He at one time was a wealthy man, but the depression of the real estate market in 1870, which continued for several succeeding years, made his financial burdens greater than he could bear, and disaster following thick and following faster, brought at last impoverishment, and a few years ago his brethren laid him away among the flowers of that other, and rapidly growing but silent city, "Mountain View."

Brother Samuel H. Robinson, the Secretary, was elected Master in 1858, serving one term. He was elected Mayor of Oakland and served the term of 1856 and 1857.

At the first meeting of the lodge in its humble and primitive lodge room, petitions were received from A. D. McDevitt, Sam. Bell McKee, H. A. Higley and F. K. Shattuck. Brother Shattuck is the only living representative of that quartet.

I find these petitions were referred to committees composed of the following brethren: Malachi Fallon, A. M. Barnard, B. L. Jones, P. Hayes, J. E. Whitcher, Solomon Beel, L. Lengfeld and J. P. M. Davis. All but one of these brethren have crossed over to the immortal shore.

On Friday evening, September 2, 1854, the second meeting of the lodge was held—same officers present, with H. C. Spicer, Treasurer; A. M Barnard, Senior Deacon; Solomon Beel, Junior Deacon and P. Hayes, Tyler.

The petitioners of the former meeting were all elected to receive the degrees. Petitions for the degrees were also received from Edson Adams and M. Parker.

At this meeting each member paid one year's dues in advance, and Sam. Bell McKee and Francis K. Shattuck were initiated Entered Apprentice Masons.

The third meeting was held September 9, at which a

ISAAC E. PADDOCK.

Petitioner for Dispensation and Charter Member.
First Master under Charter, 1885,
Deceased.

Brother Griswold acted as Senior Deacon, probably a visitor, as his name does not appear again in the records of the lodge. Also Brother Franklin Warner, our venerable Past Master, acted as Tyler.

At this meeting Most Worshipful Charles M. Radcliffe, Past Grand Master, visited the lodge, and the first degree was conferred upon A. D. McDevitt and H. A. Higley.

On September 25, Brothers McKee, Shattuck and Higley were passed to the degree of Fellow Craft.

October 7, Joseph Black and M. Parker were elected, and received the Entered Apprentice degree the same evening.

October 22, Brothers McKee and Higley were raised to the sublime degree of Master Mason—the first Master Masons made in Alameda County.

On October 28, Brother Black was made a Master Mason, the third in honor.

On November 4, petitions were received for the degrees from J. Kellersberger and D. S. Lacy, and from Brother Franklin Warner for affiliation. At this meeting Brother F. K. Shattuck received the degree of Master Mason—the fourth on the roll of honor.

At the meeting January 21, 1855, the lodge was visited by the Grand Master, William H. Howard, accompanied by Brother George J. Hobe, Master of Golden Gate Lodge, No. 30, of San Francisco. The third degree was conferred upon Brothers Parker and Lacy; and after the labors of the evening the brethren were called to refreshment, and sat down to a banquet given in honor of the visit of the Grand Master.

The last meeting held under dispensation was April 6, 1855, at which $20 was voted to the Grand Lodge fund to furnish a memorial stone for the Washington monument.

HORACE A. HIGLEY.

Born in Pensacola, Florida, about 1827
M. M. Live Oak Lodge, U. D , Oct. 22, 1854.
Was W. M. in 1856.
Died in Mobile, Alabama, about 1874

which perfect ashlar graces the now completed monument,
bearing the proper inscription: "Presented by the Masonic
Fraternity of California."

UNDER THE CHARTER.

At the annual communication of the Grand Lodge, held at
Sacramento, commencing May 1, 1855, a charter was
granted, and on May 9, the lodge was constituted, under
the title of Live Oak Lodge, No. 61, Free and Accepted
Masons. The brethren named as charter members were
as follows: Lawrence C. Owen, Isaac E. Paddock, Jeremiah
E. Whitcher, Samuel H. Robinson, Sam. Bell McKee,
Francis K. Shattuck, Joseph Black, Solomon Beel, Malachi Fallon, P. Hayes, J. P. M. Davis, A. M. Barnard, B.
L. Jones, L. Lengfeld, Franklin Warner and H. C. Spicer. Of these pioneer Masons of Alameda County only
three remain, F. K. Shattuck, Franklin Warner, and Malachi Fallon—and only two, Brothers Shattuck and Warner,
have maintained their membership in the fraternity, and
are present with us this evening.

Of the departed members I have already referred to
Brothers Owen, Paddock, Whitcher, and Robinson.
Brother Shattuck is still with us, honored and respected.
He was the first clerk of the city of Oakland, and held the
position in 1852-53-54 and 1864-65-66-67; was member
of the City Council in 1856-57-58; was Mayor of the city
in 1859-60, and Superintendent of Schools in 1862-63.
He represented the county in the State Legislature, and
held the office of Supervisor for a dozen years or more.

Sam. Bell McKee held the office of County Judge, was
for a long series of years District Judge, and was finally
promoted to the bench of the Supreme Court.

Brother H. C. Spicer died in 1856.

Brother J. P. M. Davis was City Marshal and Tax Col-

SAMUEL BELL McKEE.

Born in Black Abbey, Grey Abbey, Port Ferry, near Belfast, Ireland. Aug., 1822.

M. M. Live Oak Lodge, Oct. 22, 1854.

Was W. M. in 1857.

Died March 2, 1887.

lector in 1855-56-57-58, and Mayor in 1860-61-62.

Brother Franklin Warner was one of the early educators of this city, was School Director in 1866-67, was Councilman in 1872-73-74.

Of the balance of these pioneers I have been unable to gather data for this sketch.

On May 9, 1855, the lodge was opened by John F. Damon, Past Master of Lebanon Lodge, No. 49, Acting Master, when the following were elected the first officers under the charter: Isaac E. Paddock, Worshipful Master; Jeremiah E. Whitcher, Senior Warden; H. A Higley, Junior Warden; Samuel H. Robinson, Treasurer; Sam. B. McKee, Secretary. The following were the appointed officers: James Black, Senior Deacon; John Scott, Junior Deacon; Franklin Warner, Tyler.

One week after the constitution a meeting of the lodge was called for the purpose of taking action upon the death of the first Grand Secretary, Worshipful Levi Stowell, and the lodge resolved to attend the funeral the next day, Saturday, May 18, 1855, in a body. The services were held in San Francisco, under the direction of the Grand Lodge, and Brothers Shattuck, Robinson, Higley, and Black were appointed a committee from Live Oak Lodge to accompany the remains to San Jose, where the body was given Masonic burial.

The membership at this time was 24. There were initiated from August 16, 1854, to May 1, 1855, 10; passed 9; raised, 9. Total receipts, $888; total expenditures, $878.

The first recorded case of charity was at the meeting of the lodge September 7, 1855, when Brother Shattuck reported that Mrs. ——, a widow of a Past Grand Master of Louisiana, was in sore need. It is hardly necessary to

SAMUEL HAYWARD ROBINSON.
Born in Dudley, Mass., Nov. 16, 1825.
Petitioner for Dispensation and Charter Member.
Was W. M. in 1854.
Died Oct 24, 1875.

state that the lodge came to her relief, as it never has failed to do from that day to this in similar cases.

If there be a pleasure on earth which angels cannot enjoy, which they might almost envy man the possession of, it is the power of relieving distress, and more than angelic happiness and satisfaction lies in the disposition to relieve distress.

The first annual meeting of the lodge under its charter was held December 7, 1855, when the following officers were elected: Horace A. Higley, W. M.; Joseph Black, S. W.; S. B. McKee, J. W.; J. P. M. Davis, Treasurer; M. Evans, Sec. The installation was held on the evening of St. John the Evangelist's Day. Membership, 27.

From this period I am obliged to treat very briefly the historical events of the lodge to bring myself within the time allotted me.

At the second annual election, December 5, 1856, Sam. Bell McKee was chosen Master. In those early days promotion was not the rule. The brethren considered qualification first of importance, which was both wise and just.

On January 2 1857, the first offshoot from the lodge took place. Several brethren dimited for the purpose of forming a lodge at San Leandro, which town had become the county seat. The result was the institution of Eden Lodge, No. 113, Live Oak's first daughter.

The offshoot crippled the lodge for a time, and the next two years were years of struggle, which tested the character of the lodge and determined that it was entitled to the name, "Live Oak." And the old 'Live Oak" ship has weathered many a storm since then. And now, in her old age, still sound, staunch, and true, is sailing the peaceful and untroubled waters of prosperity in the forefront of all the lodges of this State for work unexcelled,

JEREMIAH ELKINS WHITCHER.
Born, Andover, Merrimac Co., N. H., June 13, 1817.
Petitioner for Dispensation and Charter Member.
Was W. M. in 1859.
Died Jan. 24, 1888.

character and vigor of its members, deeds of charity, and financial success.

December 5, 1857, Samuel H. Robinson was chosen Master. The returns to the Grand Lodge May, 1858, showed a membership of only 16.

At the fourth annual election, December 3, 1858, Jeremiah E. Whitcher was chosen Master, with F. K. Shattuck Senior Warden, and Judge George M. Blake Junior Warden—a strong team, and from that day the lodge took a new start on the road of prosperity.

August 6, 1859, the lodge voted the use of the lodge room for the purpose of forming a chapter of Royal Arch Masons. The result was Oakland Chapter No. 26.

The fifth annual election was held December 2, 1859, when the same officers were re-elected.

On December 23, Rev. Benj. Akerly was raised to the sublime degree of Master Mason. Father Akerly, though past his fourscore years, is still with us, honored and respected, as he deserves.

About this time the lodge treasury must have been plethoric, as a resolution was adopted authorizing the loaning of the surplus funds at two per cent interest per month.

At the meeting held April 6, 1860, the lodge appropriated $100 for relief of the needy. And these golden drops have fallen like the dews of heaven upon the violet beds, distilling perfumes of sweetness these forty long years. "We are rich only in what we give, and poor only in what we refuse" has ever been the motto of the lodge. Roll of membership 29.

The sixth annual election was held December 7, 1860, at which Brother Francis K. Shattuck was promoted to the Oriental chair and served the lodge with good judgment and

FRANCIS KITTRIDGE SHATTUCK.
Born in Crown Point, New York, March 16, 1825.
M. M. Live Oak Lodge, Nov. 4, 1854.
Was W. M. in 1861.

ability. The result was a membership of thirty-five.

At the seventh annual election, December 6, 1861, Brother George M. Blake was elected Master, and another year of good results followed.

During this year the lodge followed the tide of improvement up Broadway and moved to the brick building of Judge McKee, on the corner of Fourth Street. The lodge room was fitted up with a new carpet, pictures and a library was started.

The older brethren will remember that in May of this year the Grand Lodge laid the corner stone of the State capitol at Sacramento, when there was the largest gathering of the fraternity which had ever taken place in this State.

At the eighth annual election, December 5, 1862, Rev. Benjamin Akerly was elected Master—taken from the floor of the lodge. Membership 37.

On June 15, 1863, the lodge laid the corner stone of the new and large building for Mrs. Blake's Seminary for Young Ladies, one of the early educational institutions of the State, organized in 1858.

The ninth annual election, December, 1863, retained Father Akerly in the East. This year Alameda Lodge, No. 167, was instituted at Centerville, with 14 members—the second daughter of Live Oak Lodge.

On September 20, 1864, the lodge gave Masonic burial to Brother J. P. M. Davis, who had faithfully served the lodge as treasurer for ten years. Forty-one members were reported this year.

At the tenth annual election, December, 1864, Brother Akerly was elected to retain the gavel for the third term.

At the stated meeting, held May 5, 1865, appropriate resolutions upon the assassination of Abraham Lincoln,

GEORGE MANSFIELD BLAKE.

Born in Elizabethtown, New York, March 16, 1821
M. M. Live Oak Lodge Sept. 5, 1856.
Was W. M. in 1862.
Died Oct. 16, 1875.

the wise and revered President of this nation, its distinguished citizen and upright Mason, were unanimously adopted. Roll of membership, 50.

At the eleventh annual election, December, 1865, Brother Franklin Warner was called to the chair and ably presided over the lodge. Brother Warner is still with us, an honored and respected member. Membership 53.

November 22, 1866, the lodge again moved, occupying Shattuck Hall, corner of Broadway and Eighth Streets, and $100 was appropriated to fit up the lodge room.

The twelfth annual election, December, 1866, called Brother James O. Miner to the Master's chair.

During this administration the first movement was made for the erection of a Masonic Temple. The result was the incorporation of the Masonic Fund Association—through which, twelve years later, Live Oak Lodge took one-tenth of the stock of the present Masonic Temple Association—and at the present time owns one-sixth of the stock. Number of members, 59.

At the thirteenth annual election, December 6, 1867, Brother James Lentell was chosen Master—one of the few Past Masters left and the most faithful attendant at lodge meetings of all its members.

At the stated meeting, February 7, 1868, a petition from Brother N. W. Spaulding and thirteen other brethren was presented, asking the lodge to recommend the granting of a dispensation for the formation of Oakland Lodge (now 188), which petition was granted and the use of the lodge room tendered this third daughter of the mother lodge Number of members this year, 64.

At the fourteenth annual election, December, 1868, Brother James C. Kyte was chosen Master. His administration was marked for the amount of work done. Dur-

FRANKLIN WARNER.

Born in Pittsford, Rutland Co., Vermont, Sept. 16, 1818.
M. M. Miami Lodge, Piqua, Miami Co., Ohio, Dec., 1841.
Was W. M. in 1866.

ing one month there were eight called meetings for work. Number of members this year, 77.

The fifteenth annual election, December 3, 1869, honored Brother Kyte with a re-election.

In March, 1870, the lodge through the Masonic Fund Association, and in its name, purchased the property on the northeast corner of Tenth and Franklin Streets, 100x 62½ feet, which property was sold three years ago at an advance of some $20,000. Number of members this year, 90.

At the sixteenth annual election, December 2, 1870, Brother Thatcher P. Wales was chosen Master.

On March 3, 1871, the lodge adopted a resolution recommending the organization of a lodge at Alameda—afterwards christened Oak Grove, No. 215—the fourth daughter of the mother lodge. Number of members 99.

At the seventeenth annual election December 1, 1871, Brother Wales was re-elected Master.

At the stated meeting, March 1, 1872, the use of the lodge room, free of rent for six months was granted to Oak Leaf Chapter, No. 8, Order of the Eastern Star, which had just been organized. October 4 of the same year, Brother Henry Cooms donated to the lodge a beautiful altar—the same altar which now graces the lodge room in this temple. At the stated meeting, December 6, 1872, seventeen brethren residing in East Oakland—then called the town of Brooklyn—asked for recommendation for dispensation to form a lodge, which was granted, and the fifth daughter was instituted and christened Brooklyn Lodge, No. 225. The number of members this year, 107.

At the eighteenth annual election, December 6, 1872, the lodge honored Brother Wales by continuing him in the Master's chair for the third term. Number of members this year, 119.

JAMES OGDEN MINER.

Born in Hartford, Conn., Jan. 28, 1835
M. M. Live Oak Lodge, Sept. 7, 1860.
Was W. M. in 1867.

At the nineteenth annual election, December, 1873, Brother Wales was again re-elected Master. But after six months' service, he was called away, and there being a vacancy in the office of Senior Warden, under dispensation from the Grand Master, a special election was held August 5, 1874, and Brother James C. Martin was elected to fill the unexpired term of Master. Number of members 118.

At the twentieth annual election, December 3, 1874, Brother Martin was continued in the Master's chair, and under his adm'nistration the membership increased to 127.

At the twenty-first annual election, December 3, 1875, Brother H. B. Pomroy was chosen Master.

October 6, 1876, the lodge granted the petition of thirty brethren of West Oakland for the institution of a lodge, and a sixth daughter was christened Alcatraz Lodge, No. 244. Number of members this year, 128.

At the twenty-second annual election, December 1, 1876, Brother James T. Gardiner was called to the East. Number of members, 124.

At the twenty-third annual election, December 7, 1877, Brother John C. Marsh was chosen Master.

June 7, 1878, a committee of the lodge appointed for the purpose reported in favor of the building of a Masonic Temple—all of the bodies of Masonry of Central Oakland acting in unison. The lodge voted to subscribe for 1,000 of the 10,000 shares of the capital stock. Membership, 113.

At the twenty-fourth annual election, December 6, 1878, Brother John R. Glascock was called to the East. Membership, 104.

At the twenty-fifth annual election, December 5, 1879,

JAMES LENTELL.

Born near Waltham, Middlesex Co., Mass., Oct. 6, 1818.
M. M. Live Oak Lodge, Jan. 21, 1859.
Was W. M. in 1868.

Brother James C. Martin was again returned to the Master's chair.

January 10, 1880, the corner stone of this temple was laid by the Grand Lodge. In the sealed receptacle placed in the cavity prepared for that purpose was a list of the charter members, historical sketch and names of all the members of this lodge. Membership, 103.

At the twenty-sixth annual election, December 3, 1880, Brother Martin was again elected to wield the gavel for the fourth term. The first stated meeting after the election, February 4, 1881, was held in the new temple, it having been duly dedicated by the Grand Lodge, assisted by delegations from all the grand bodies of Masonry, and a multitude of the Sons of Light from different sections of the State. Membership, 110.

At the twenty-seventh annual election, December 2, 1881, Brother John A. Mattingly was chosen Master. Membership, 105.

At the twenty-eighth annual election, December, 1882, Brother Robert J. Beeby was chosen Master. Brother Beeby was an efficient officer, a good and true man, and an upright Mason. He passed to his reward only a few months ago. This year the roll showed 112 members.

At the twenty-ninth annual election, December 7, 1883, Brother Beeby was continued Master. During this administration the Masonic Board of Relief was organized by a compact, dated August 29, 1884, between Live Oak Lodge and Oakland Lodge—and for nearly four years these two lodges, unaided, maintained the board alone—when, on April 4, 1888, Brooklyn Lodge joined in the compact. Roll of members this year showed 118.

At the thirtieth annual election, December 5, 1884, Brother Edward C. Robinson was chosen Master. Membership, 115.

JAMES CARTER KYTE.

Born in Geneva, Ontario Co., New York, Sept. 29, 1833.
M. M. Live Oak Lodge, Nov. 3, 1859.
Was W. M. in 1869-70.

At the thirty-first annual election, December 4, 1885. Brother Henry P. Dalton was called to the chair.

During the year the lodge held a series of meetings for the delivery of essays upon Masonic literature and kindred topics, which were very interesting and instructive. During the month of October the lodge held seven called meetings for work, and five called meetings for work were held in November, besides work at the stated meetings. Membership, 118.

At the thirty-second annual election, December 3, 1886, Brother W. Francis Perry was chosen Master. The roll of membership showed 136.

At the thirty-third annual election, December 1, 1887, Brother Marcus D. Hyde was called to the chair. The roll of membership showed 143.

At the thirty-fourth annual election, December, 1888, Brother Perry was again called to preside. Membership, 159.

At the thirty-fifth annual election, December, 1889, Brother Perry was again re-elected. Membership, 174.

At the thirty-sixth annual election, December, 1890, Brother Harry C. Bush was called to preside. This exceeded all the previous years, save one, in gain of membership. The roll showed 193.

At the thirty-seventh annual election, December, 1891. Brother Frank N. Dalton was chosen Master. Prosperity still continued. Membership, 203.

At the thirty-eighth annual election, December, 1892, Brother Junia J. Warner was called to preside. Again the lodge forged ahead. Membership, 213.

At the thirty-ninth annual election, December, 1893. Brother Charles E. Haven, the present Master, was chosen.

THATCHER PETER WALES.

Born in Syracuse, N. Y., Feb. 5, 1824.
Was W. M. in 1871-72-73-74.
Died Sept. 22, 1893.

The lodge has been visited by death so far this year five times, taking three Past Masters. Roll of membership at date, 212.

The fortieth annual election will occur next December.

The lodge has had forty elections under the charter, but the first election was held, at its institution in May, 1855, while the first annual election occurred the following December. There have been elected twenty-nine Masters of the lodge, of whom ten have passed from earth; and nineteen are still living, all of whom are residing in Oakland save one, Brother Mattingly, now living in Fresno.

The Daughters of Live Oak Lodge are: Eden, No. 113, San Leandro, instituted May 14, 1857; Alameda, 167, Centerville, October 13, 1864; Oakland, 188, Oakland, October 15, 1868; Oak Grove, 215, Alameda, October 14, 1871; Mosaic, 218, Livermore, October 11, 1872; Brooklyn, 225, East Oakland, October 28, 1873; Eucalyptus, 243, Haywards, October 12, 1876; Alcatraz, 244, West Oakland, October 11, 1877; Durant, 268, Berkeley, October 11, 1883, and the baby daughter, Alisal, under dispensation, Pleasanton, born July 17, 1894.

And between these daughters and the mother lodge the most fraternal harmony and good will prevails. And in the name of the mother lodge I extend to her daughters the motherly greeting of good fellowship and that maternal love and kindness that good daughters deserve. And may it ever be said of you, " Behold how good and how pleasant it is for daughters to dwell together in unity."

HORACE BARTON POMROY.

Born in Springfield. Mass., Nov. 17, 1816.
M M. Carson Lodge, No. 1, Carson City, Nev., March 13, 1866.
Was W. M. in 1876.
Died Jan. 20, 1883.

M. M. Estee Discourses on the Good Accomplished.

PAST GRAND MASTER MORRIS M. ESTEE, having been invited to visit the lodge and make an address, said:—

I believe in Masonry as one of the civilizing and one of the Christianizing institutions of the country. It has survived through many centuries, until now it is practically universal. It is known in every country and its rituals are repeated in every tongue.

It is said that age gives knowledge to man. If that be so with man in the brief period of his existence, what must be the effect upon an institution like Masonry, which lives through all the centuries? A distinguished religionist was once asked what he could say to prove that the Christian religion was what it purported to be, and that Christ had come to the world and died to save sinners. He was not a learned man in religious controversy, but with the promptness and the generous impulse of one whose faith was born in love and inspired by the great Supreme Ruler, he said: "The Christian religion has lived eighteen hundred years, and it has improved the condition of mankind every year of its existence. There are more Christians to-day than ever before. It has saved the souls of countless millions, and never wronged a single human being."

For similar but less potential reasons we say the antiquity of Masonry, the fact that it has never injured a human being, that it has benefited and exalted the human character, shows that it is one of the grandest and the most beneficent of human institutions. Masonry is indeed a colossal edifice, erected only for the purpose of benefiting the distressed of this life. Its chief ambition and greatest achievements have been to make men happier and better.

I remember a legend of a rich man who had three sons, and who was in doubt as to which one to make his heir. He called the three to him, and addressing the eldest, asked what he would most like to accomplish in this life. The son replied that it would be his ambition to be the greatest general in the world—to conquer the whole world and to establish empires. Upon the second son being asked the same question, he replied that his ambition would be to accumulate wealth, create commerce, construct ships and be the greatest merchant the world had ever known. The father finally turned to the youngest and asked, "What would be your ambition?" He replied: "I do not want to conquer the world; by doing that I would have to injure someone. I do no want to accumulate vast wealth, as by doing that I must unjustly take the property of others. My ambition would be gratified if I could dry up the tears of sorrow, if I could relieve the wants of the needy, if I could feed the hungry and comfort the distressed and bury the dead." And upon him the father conferred his name and wealth.

This to me seems to be an instructive lesson, showing to us that our first duty is to others, our last to ourselves. This is the mission of Masonry. And yet we must admit that, being a human institution, many bad men may be members thereof; but it could be truly said that every man who is a Mason is better for being such.

Although Masonry is as old as civilization, yet every day of its existence presents new light to both old and young Masons. If it is old it is so only in the same sense that a devoted son's mother was old to him when he said that he saw nothing but perpetual youth in her face. He noted none of the wrinkles which to others marked the approach of age. He only fathomed the depths of her soul, and read over and over again in his own recollection the beauty of her life. He saw again her motherly devotion to him when a child, her Christian spirit, which had given inspiration to her whole life, and so he said, and truly too, that she might be old in years, but to him she would be always young.

JAMES TODD GARDINER.
Born in Leeds, Yorkshire, England, May 9, 1835.
M. M. Live Oak Lodge, March 20, 1874.
Was W. M. in 1877.

Address of Bro. David L. Smoot.

MASONRY, ITS CARDINAL VIRTUES.

THE Cardinal Virtues of Masonry was the theme assigned to Brother David L. Smoot, who substantially said:—

Ladies, Friends, and Brethren: It has been said that this ancient order originally traveled through the civilized world, erecting temples, cathedrals, and churches by the aid of a mystic art that so exactly prepared each stone at the far-distant quarry for its particular place in the rising structure, that no waste material was transported, and the polished ashlars were lifted into place without change or the sound of hammer.

In those days, Masons were brown-handed sons of toil, practicing the cardinal virtues of temperance, fortitude, prudence and justice, and though the order has passed from the hard lines of operative or practical Masonry to the delicate refinements of speculative or theoretical Masonry, yet, in obedience to hallowed tradition, the order is not deaf to the plea of labor or blind to its sacred rights, nor does it cease to cultivate temperance, fortitude, prudence, and justice.

The order is to each member what the home place and the home friends are to the traveler. A great soldier, as distinguished guest, passed around the world in a glow of national hospitality, but it is said that he never really

47

JOHN CARLTON MARSH.

Born in Petersburg, Menard Co., Illinois, Oct. 21, 1848.
M. M. Live Oak Lodge, April 11, 1873.
Was W. M. in 1878

smiled until he reached the home place and the home friends of Galena.

> It was his lodge, a place of repose,
> A refuge of friends, a refuge from foes.

Another great soldier, with the wreckage of disaster strewn hopelessly about him, and the future confronting as a starless night, was asked by one of his fearless lieutenants what would become of them. With a placid grandeur born of something more than mortal, he replied: "Surely human virtue is equal to human calamity." He was a Mason, and this was fortitude.

Address of Bro. H. P. McPike.

WORSHIPFUL MASTER, LADIES AND GENTLEMEN: It has fallen to my lot to be required to participate in these exercises to the extent of having something to say in behalf of the fair sex. It is customary for all extempore speakers to come prepared for the occasion, and I have not departed from this in the least. I have in my pocket a manuscript, with the contents of which it is my purpose to inflict you, and I wish to say at the outset that such a course is the result of wilful and deliberate premeditation on my part. Most any attorney at law ought to be able to talk a great deal and say very little on the shortest notice, but I do not propose to permit any temerity I may possess in this regard to betray me into an opportunity to allow my mind to run riot and wanton with an unbridled tongue upon so delicate a subject as "the ladies."

You may find during the course of my written remarks that I have reached after some witticisms. If you should happen to discover that particular part, and do not feel that it stirs you up to any sudden flood of mirth, just consider how different it might have sounded had I spoken it with an air of spontaniety, as if it had occurred to me on the moment, instead of reading it to you. Wit should

50

come forth like the bursting of a fountain from the earth, in original, natural force, so say the critics.

But one of the accredited wittiest men of history is Richard Brindsley Sheridan. He was so witty that his shafts often penetrated a London fog, and wrinkled the face and shook the sides of the stolid Briton. He was a lawyer, and when he died, as is frequently the case, his entire estate was found to consist of papers. When these papers were examined by his creditors, it was found that his famous witticisms did not spring full-armed from his intellect, like Minerva from the head of Jove, but had been gradually evolved, like the human race from one of Mr. Darwin's monkeys.

Besides the witty portion of my address, you will observe, if you pay close attention, that I have not committed myself upon anything. In fine, as I said before, this subject is an "edged tool," and any man who ventures to handle it is but a child. I have, therefore, carefully abstained from saying anything which I will have to take back, and I don't propose to take back anything I haven't said; so, with these few premonitory remarks I will, with your kind attention, read what I have written.

Inasmuch as it is the 40th anniversary of the birth of our lodge that we are celebrating to-night, I do not propose to go further back in the past than that number of years for any personal reminiscences which I may have to offer, and as it is never considered polite to call the attention of ladies to matters which occurred early in their lives, I shall not pain even the youngest here by again referring to what happened in eighteen hundred and fifty-four.

You will pardon me if I appear a little ill at ease this evening, for I never found myself in quite this predicament before. I am expected to discourse to you about "our

JOHN ANDREW MATTINGLY.
Born in Jackson, Miss., July 12, 1852.
M. M. Live Oak Lodge, Dec. 2, 1881.
Was W. M. in 1882.

mothers, our sisters, our daughters, our wives and our widows.'' Just how a man can be a good Mason and talk about his own widow, is a problem I do not care to explain, therefore, if I happen to slight my own widow in these remarks, please excuse me on the plea of the weakness of human nature, and extend to her your quiet sympathy.

Ladies, Masonry was organized for several purposes, chief among which was to give you an object lesson—to teach you that man can keep a secret. It was also organized to keep your curiosity aroused. We Masons know that just as soon as the ladies find out what we are up to all curiosity will die a natural death.

Let me tell you, ladies, Masonry was organized by King Solomon. King Solomon was the wisest of all men, and probably the most benevolently disposed. It is a cardinal principle of the order, to make provisions for the widows of the members. It is related of King Solomon that he expected to have no less than seven hundred widows, and looking down the vista of time, he imagined that it would be just the thing to have them taken care of; therefore, he organized the first Lodge of Masons.

Brother Masons, I appeal to you ! There are objects in nature which, when we contemplate them, excite in our breasts so much awe and reverence that in their presence speech feels herself rebuked, and we remain silent and contemplative, unwilling or unable to break the spell by making vocal the delicious sentiments which they awaken.

The broad, restless ocean, supporting on her bosom the vaulted heavens; the mountain peaks, receiving the earliest kisses of the dawn, or holding upon their summits the last lingering rays of departing day; the angry thun-

ROBERT JOHN BEEBY.

Born in Central Square, Oswego Co., New York, Jan. 24, 1849,
M. M. Central Square Lodge, No. 622, Sept., 1870.
Was W. M in 1883–84.
Died May 28, 1894.

derbolt fraught with heaven's artillery; the genial sunshine, giving to the earth its hues and to the sky its tints—all, all of these, turn the mind in upon itself, and hold it enchanted and voiceless. This is our experience while viewing inanimate grandeur. What must it be when we come to consider the "last reserved of God," the newest creature in the universe, lovely woman! You can better imagine than I describe. The world owes her a debt of gratitude which can never be paid. It owes its civilization to her. She rode the crest of every wave of progress which has swept over the conditions of man, from the day when he stood clothed in nothing but the hillsides, and with no covering for his head but the sky, down to the day when he was able to read the history of creation in those hills, and weigh the stars that blaze in the "canopy of heaven."

In verification of this, I might cite you to many illustrious women from the pages of history, whose names and characters tower above the age in which they lived, like a church steeple above the houses in a large city. I might look around me and point to women in our own day, who are far in advance of even this age of progress, but it is not of them I would speak, they are standing in the gaze of a nation. But those of whom I do speak, are our own mothers, our sisters, our daughters and our wives—our everyday home people right here in Oakland. There are among them many whose daily acts of goodness, whose bravery in time of trouble, whose devotedness, fortitude and self-sacrifice if published to the world would place them beside the acknowledged heroines of the earth. What man is there here present who has a wife, a mother or a sister, who can gainsay my words? What widow is

EDWARD CONSTANT ROBINSON.
Born near Jacksonville, Jackson Co., Or., Feb. 6, 1855.
M. M. Live Oak Lodge, July 22, 1881.
Was W. M. in 1885.

there among you who cannot say that if her husband
had but taken her advice in many things pertaining to his
health and welfare, her widowhood would have been
postponed to a later period of her life.

How triumphantly forgiving she looks when she says,
"I told you so," and how disastrously meek we feel when,
standing amidst the wreck and ruin of blasted hopes, we
are compelled to acknowledge that she did.

Ladies, Live Oak Lodge greets you, and feels herself
honored by your presence. It is proud of you. Her members love you. Basking in your smiles, encouraged by
your words, sustained and soothed by your loving, tender
sympathy, we feel that all the clouds which may gather
over the heads of any of our members will surely "roll by"
—that life is anything but a failure; home a comfort, and
God's latest gift the greatest boon to the world.

JOHN RAGLAND GLASCOCK.
Born in Panola Co., Miss., Aug. 25, 1845.
M. M. Live Oak Lodge, July 9, 1875,
Was W. M. in 1879.

Closing Address or Good Night.

BY PAST MASTER JOHN R. GLASCOCK.

LADIES, BRETHREN, AND FRIENDS: Every selection made in carrying out these exercises has its undoubted fitness. It was difficult at first to see the appropriateness of placing so young a man as myself at the end of the program, but events have proved the wisdom of the committee. It was not unfitting that our *youthful* Brother Martin should stand at the gates of sunrise to give you greeting, that the meridian sun of Brother Estee should disclose to you the beauties of Masonry, and that in the west the contemporary of those who have passed from us to join the silent majority on the other shore should linger to say "good night." If I did not see the justice of my selection at first, I see it now. I thought I was young; I find myself a running mate with the past.

What a flood of half-forgotten memories came in upon me at the reading of the history of our lodge! Names linked with the founding and growth of our city, names associated with honor and held in loving remembrance by friends as well as brethren, carried me back to the times when Oakland was a park shaded by oaks and carpeted with wild flowers, where now stately buildings rear their fronts—Davis, Black, Higley, McKee, and a host of others too numerous to mention. I knew them all. Good men they were in the lodge and out of it; and who shall

REV. BENJAMIN AKERLY.
Born in New York City, Oct. 28, 1812
M. M. Live Oak Lodge, Dec. 23, 1859.
Was W. M. in 1863-64-65.

say that they were not better men for being good Masons?
It was not given to all of them to stand in the prominent
walks of life, but each in his own way wrought out a life
squared with the principles of his order, and the sum of
their efforts has gone to build up and beautify humanity.
Their lives have taught us that if there is any one principle that, more than another, typifies the true spirit of
Masonry, that lifts human life out of the rut of commer-
cial accommodation into a broader touch with humanity
and a closer communion with the divine, it is human love.
This is the sum and the essence of Masonry, and the
Mason who has lifted the veil and failed to interpret this
inscription written in words of fire upon his lodge's altar
has failed to grasp the full sublimity of Masonic teaching.
Do not understand that the words "human love" are used
in any restricted sense. It is not that love which gives
for a return, but that which gives because it is right to
give and because it cannot help giving, and which grows
richer and stronger for the giving—such a love as Mrs.
Browning spoke of when she said—

"Thy love
Shall chant itself its own beatitudes
After its own life working. A child's kiss
Set on thy sighing lips shall make thee glad;
A poor man served by thee shall make thee rich;
A sick man helped by thee shall make thee strong;
Thou shalt be served thyself by every sense
Of service which thou renderest."

With such love woven into the fiber of its being, Masonry cannot die. Its sun, risen upon so boundless a field
of divine activity, not all the starry hosts of time, not all the
glory spaces of eternity, can say to Masonry "good night."

The entertainment was closed by the venerable
Dr. Akerly, Past Master of the lodge, leading the audi-
ence standing in a recital of the Lord's prayer, and then
dismissing it with a benediction.

Past Master's Jewel.
Live Oak Lodge. No. 61

Dispensation.

Granted by Grand Master W. H. Howard to institute Live Oak Lodge, U. D., on August 16, 1854. The following named brethren signed the petition for dispensation, and met and organized August 19, 1854:—

*L. C. Owen.   *Patrick Hayes.
*I. E. Paddock.   *L. Lengfeld.
*J. E. Whitcher.   *H. C. Spicer.
*S. H. Robinson.   *B. L. Jones.
*Malachi Fallon.   *E. Alexander.
*A. M. Barnard.   *Solomon Beel.
                *Wm. T. Brown.

* Not now members.

Charter granted May 4, 1855. Signed by—

W. H. Howard, G. M.   R. N. Wood, J. G. W.
N. Greene Curtis, D. G. M. Adelison Martin, G. Treas.
R. E. Cole, S. G. W.   L. Stowell, G. S.

LIST OF NAMES ON CHARTER OF LIVE OAK LODGE.

†L. C. Owen.   F. Warner.
†I. E. Paddock.   *M. Fallon.
†J. E. Whitcher.   †P. Hayes
†S. H. Robinson.   †J. P. M. Davis.
†S. B. McKee.   †A. M. Barnard.
†J. Black.   †B. L. Jones.
†S. Beel.   †L. Lengfeld.
                †H. C. Spicer.

* Not now member.   † Deceased.

JAS. SHAKESPEARE, S. Stew.   O. K. STAMPLEY, Tyler   W. G. MANUEL, S. D.

J. W. NELSON, J. D.   J. I. WARNSER, Sec.   H. G. HUNT, Organist.   J. P. Imhoff, Mar

E. H. HART, J. W.   C. E. HAYES, W. M.   J. A. BECKWITH, S. W.   W. F. BLOOR, Treas

REV. GEO. W. SWEENY, Chaplain.   N. A. PARRISH, J. Stew.

PAST MASTERS OF LIVE OAK LODGE, NO. 61.

†Lawrence C. Owen, 1854.

†Isaac E. Paddock, 1855.

†Horace A. Higley, 1856.

†Samuel B. McKee, 1857.

†Samuel H. Robinson, 1858.

†Jeremiah E. Whitcher, 1859, '60.

Francis K. Shattuck, 1861.

†Geo. M. Blake, 1862.

Benjamin Akerly, 1863, '64, '65.

Franklin Warner, 1866.

James O. Miner, 1867.

James Lentell, 1868.

James C. Kyte, 1869, '70.

†Thatcher P. Wales, 1871, '72, '73, '74.

James C. Martin, 1875, '80, '81.

†Henry B. Pomroy, 1876.

James T. Gardiner, 1877.

John C. Marsh, 1878.

John R Glascock, 1879.

*John A. Mattingly, 1882.

†Robert J. Beeby, 1883, '84

Edward C. Robinson, 1885.

Henry P. Dalton, 1886.

*W. Francis Perry, 1887, '89, '90.

Marcus D. Hyde, 1888.

Harry C. Bush, 1891.

Frank N. Dalton, 1892.

Junia J. Warner, 1893.

Charles E. Haven, 1894.

* Not now members.   † Deceased.

HENRY PHILIP DALTON.
Born in Jacksonville, Tuolumne Co., Cal., April 27, 1860
M. M. Live Oak Lodge, Sept. 22, 1882.
Was W. M. in 1886.

Past Masters by Affiliation.

Amasa W. Bishop.
Frank H. Brooks.
Nelson Carr.
Noble Hamilton.
William R. Hatfield.
Julius Samuels.

First Officers under the Charter.

Lodge Constituted, May 9, 1855.

Isaac E. Paddock, W. M.
Jeremiah E. Whitcher, S. W.
Horace A. Higley, J. W.
Samuel H. Robinson, Treas.
Samuel B. McKee, Sec.
James Black, S. D.
John Scott, J. D.
Franklin Warner, Tyler.

Officers 1894.

Charles E. Haven, W. M.
John A. Beckwith, S. W.
Edward H. Hart, J. W.
William F. Blood, Treas
Junia J. Warner, Sec.
George W. Sweeney, Chaplain
James P. Edoff, Marshal.
Walter G. Manuel, S. D.
James W. Nelson, J. D.
James Shakespeare, S. S.
Norman A. Parrish, J. S.
Henry O. Hunt, Organist.
Orville K. Stampley, Tyler.

MARCUS DARIUS HYDE.
Born in Jamaica, West Indies (of American parents) May 14, 1849.
M. M. Live Oak Lodge, Nov. 23, 1883.
Was W. M. in 1888.

Honorary Life Members.

Benjamin Akerly.
Samuel Bookstaver Bell.
Amasa Wright Bishop.
Frank Howard Brooks.
James Lentell.
Francois Reinstadler.
Franklin Warner.

EXPLANATORY.

In March, 1870, this lodge purchased a lot on the northeast corner of Tenth and Franklin Streets, going in debt for a portion of the purchase price of same.

Later a committee was appointed to devise measures by which the lodge could free itself from debt, and the action of this committee resulted in the incorporation August 17, 1871, of the Masonic Fund Association. Its object was to represent and protect the interests of this lodge, in the property standing in the name of said Masonic Fund Association.

This Fund Association is in existence to this date and this lodge is the owner in fact of all its stock.

In March, 1891 the above lot was sold and the Association (which is the lodge) is now free from debt, and its assets are as follows:—

ASSETS.

Oakland Masonic Temple Association Stock...$16,330 00
Certificate of Deposit in Central Bank, Cash.. 6,900 00
Note of J. T. Gulick, Secured by Mortgage.... 1,000 00

Total Assets of the Lodge held by
Masonic Fund Association..$24,230 00

The income from above is now being paid into the treasury of the lodge, and is used for current expenses.

By=Laws of

Live Oak Lodge, No 61

Adopted at its stated meeting, July 7, 1893.

ARTICLE I.

NAME AND OFFICERS.

SECTION 1. This Lodge shall be known by the name of LIVE OAK LODGE, No. 61, of Free and Accepted Masons, and its officers shall consist of a Master, a Senior Warden, a Junior Warden, a Treasurer, a Secretary, a Senior Deacon, a Junior Deacon, a Marshal, two Stewards, a Tyler, and such other officers as the Lodge may deem proper to appoint.

ARTICLE II.

ELECTIONS AND APPOINTMENTS.

SECTION 1. The Master, the Senior and Junior Wardens, the Treasurer, and the Secretary shall be elected by ballot, in conformity with Section 1, Article I, Part IV, of the Constitution of the Grand Lodge. The other officers shall be appointed by the Master, except the Junior Deacon, who may be appointed by the Senior Warden.

ARTICLE III.

MEETINGS OF THE LODGE.

SECTION 1. The stated meetings of this Lodge shall be held on the first Friday in each month.

SEC. 2. Special meetings may be called from time to time as the Lodge, or the presiding officer thereof, may direct.

ARTICLE IV.

INITIATION AND MEMBERSHIP.

SECTION I. All petitions for initiation or affiliation must be signed by the petitioner and be recommended by two members of the Lodge. Every such petition shall be referred to a committee of three, whose duty it shall be to report thereon at the next stated meeting (unless further time be granted), when the applicant shall be balloted for and received or rejected.

SEC. 2. If an applicant, elected to receive the degrees in this Lodge, does not come forward to be initiated within three months thereafter, the fee shall be forfeited, unless the Lodge shall otherwise direct.

SEC. 3. Every person raised to the degree of Master Mason in this Lodge (except when such degree shall have been conferred at the *request* of another Lodge), or elected to be a member thereof, shall sign its By-Laws.

ARTICLE V.

THE TREASURER.

SECTION I. The Treasurer shall receive all moneys from the Secretary, shall keep an accurate and just account thereof, and shall pay the same out only upon an order duly signed by the Master, and countersigned by the Secretary. He shall, at the stated meetings in June and December of each year, submit a report in full of the monetary transactions of the Lodge. The Lodge may also, at any time when considered necessary, cause him to present an account of his receipts and disbursements, and of the amount of funds on hand.

HARRY CHARLES BUSH.

Born in Erie, Pa., May 12, 1858.
M. M. Live Oak Lodge, Dec. 2, 1886.
Was W. M. in 1891.
Now Grand Lecturer of the Grand Lodge.

SEC. 2. He shall, if required by the Lodge, execute a good and sufficient bond to the Master, for the faithful performance of his duties.

ARTICLE VI.

THE SECRETARY.

SECTION I. The Secretary shall keep a faithful record of all proceedings proper to be written; shall transmit a copy of the same to the Grand Lodge when required; shall keep a separate account for each member of the Lodge; shall report, at the stated meetings in June and December of each year, the amounts due by each; shall receive all moneys due the Lodge, and pay the same monthly to the Treasurer; and shall perform all such other duties as may properly appertain to his office.

SEC. 2. He shall receive such compensation for his services as the Lodge may direct; and shall, if required by the Lodge, execute a good and sufficient bond to the Master for the faithful performance of his duties.

ARTICLE VII.

THE TYLER.

SECTION I. The Tyler, in addition to the necessary duties of his office, shall serve all notices and summons, and perform such other services as may be required of him by the Lodge.

SEC. 2. He shall receive such compensation for his services as the Lodge may direct.

ARTICLE VIII.

FEES.

SECTION I. The table of fees for this Lodge shall be as follows: For the three degrees, the sum of fifty dollars; for

FRANK NORRIS DALTON.
Born in Pacheco, Contra Costa Co., Cal., March 25, 1863.
M. M. Live Oak Lodge, Oct. 16, 1885.
Was W. M. in 1892.

degrees of Fellow Craft and Master Mason, when the first
degree shall have been received in another Lodge, a sum
sufficient to make a total of fifty dollars, but not less than
twenty-five dollars; for the degree of Master Mason, when
the first and second degrees shall have been received in
another Lodge, a sum sufficient to make a total of fifty
dollars, but not less than ten dollars; and for affiliation,
the sum of ten dollars.

SEC. 2.   The fee for each of the foregoing shall accompany the several petitions or applications, else they shall
not be presented by the Secretary to the Lodge.

ARTICLE IX.

DUES.

SECTION 1.   The dues of each member of this Lodge
shall be six dollars per annum, payable quarterly in advance.

SEC. 2.   No member who shall be in arrears for dues
at the time of the annual election shall be permitted to
vote, or shall be eligible to any office.

SEC. 3.   Any member who shall have been suspended
for nonpayment of his dues shall be restored to membership upon payment of all arrearages within two years
from date of suspension.

SEC. 4.   Any member who shall have been suspended
for non-payment of his dues for two years or more, shall
not be restored by payment of arrearages, or having his
dues remitted by the Lodge, except by the votes of three-
fourths of the members present at any stated meeting.

SEC. 5.   Any member in good standing may withdraw
from membership by paying his dues and notifying the
Lodge to that effect at a stated meeting, but no recom-
mendatory certificate shall be issued to him unless ordered
by the Lodge.

JUNIA JOSIAH WARNER.
Born in Almena, Van Buren Co., Mich. Aug. 2, 1860.
M. M. Live Oak Lodge, Feb. 8, 1889.
Was W. M. in 1893.
Now Secretary.

ARTICLE X.

COMMITTEES.

SECTION 1. The Master and Wardens shall be a Charity Committee, and shall have power to draw upon the Treasurer for any sum not exceeding ten dollars at any one time, for the relief of a distressed worthy brother, his wife, widow, or orphans.

SEC. 2. The Master, at the stated meeting next succeeding his installation, shall appoint an auditing committee, whose duty it shall be to examine all accounts presented against the Lodge.

SEC. 3. All reports of committees shall be made in writing.

ARTICLE XI.

REVEALING THE TRANSACTIONS OF THE LODGE.

SECTION 1. When a candidate for initiation or affiliation is rejected, or a brother reprimanded, suspended, or expelled, no member or visitor shall reveal, either directly or indirectly, to such person, or to any other, any transactions which may have taken place on the subject; nor shall any proceeding of the Lodge, not proper to be made public, be disclosed outside thereof, under the penalty of reprimand, suspension, or expulsion, as the Lodge may determine.

ARTICLE XII.

ORDER OF BUSINESS.

SECTION 1. The regular order of business at every stated meeting of this Lodge shall be as follows: 1. Reading of the minutes. 2. Reports of committees. 3. Ballotings. 4. Reception of petitions. 5. Miscellaneous and unfinished business. 6. Conferring degrees.

ARTICLE XIII.

SECTION 1. These By-Laws, so far as relates to the times of meeting and the amounts of fees, dues, and disbursements by the Charity Committee, may be amended at any stated meeting, by the votes of two-thirds of the members present; *provided* that notice of such amendment shall have been given at the stated meeting next preceding; but such amendment shall have no effect until approved by the Grand Lodge or Grand Master, and until such approval shall have been transmitted to the Grand Secretary.

Standing Resolutions.

Resolved, That any member having paid monthly dues to date may thereafter, upon the payment of the sum of one hundred dollars ($100) become a Life Member of this Lodge, receive a certificate to that effect signed by the Secretary under seal of the Lodge, and shall be forever freed from dues.

Resolved, That the expense in the matter of refreshments and music in all degrees, be left to the discretion of the Master and Wardens of this Lodge, who shall act as a Standing Committee, and their action thereon shall be final unless reversed by a two-thirds vote of the members present at any stated meeting.

Resolved, That a Standing Committee of three be appointed by the Master at the Stated Meeting in January of each year (to include the Secretary) to whom all subject matters of delinquent dues be referred, who may report at any stated meeting with recommendations to the Lodge as to what should be done in individual cases they have investigated.

WHEREAS, It is the duty of this Lodge to elect annually, seven of its members as Trustees of the Masonic Fund Association; therefore, be it

Resolved, That four of such Trustees be its Master, Senior and Junior Wardens and Secretary elected at the annual meeting in December, and the other three Trustees be chosen as usual from the body of the Lodge. Be it further

Resolved, That the Trustees be instructed to elect as Secretary of the Masonic Fund Association the Secretary of this Lodge, and the salary of said officer as Secretary for both offices, shall be two hundred and forty dollars per year, payable from the funds of the Lodge.

Roll of Members.

*Alexander, E................................A. Aug. 19, 1854
Akerly, Benjamin...........................Dec. 23, 1859
*Ash, Herman...............................A. April 1, 1864
*Alexander, Henry..........................A April 2, 1869
*Andresen, Harold Sophus ....Jan. 22, 1875
Andrus, Washbourne Royal............. . Jan. 31, 1879
*Atkinson, William ....A. Jan. 6, 1882
Atkinson, Thomas Albion...................A. Jan. 4, 1889
Arper, Geo. Washington ....April 19, 1889
Akerly, James Clark Smith.................Nov. 29, 1889
Avery, Mark Herbert ....A. May 5, 1893

*Beel, Solomon.............................A. Aug. 19, 1854
*Brown, Wm T..............................A. Aug. 19, 1854
*Barnard, A M.............................A. Aug. 19, 1854
*Black, Joseph ....Oct. 28, 1854
*Blake, Geo. Mansfield ....Sept. 5, 1856
Bell, Samuel Bookstaver...................A. Oct. 3, 1856
*Beal, Samuel ....A. Mar. 4, 1859
*Bingham, Joseph ....Oct. 19, 1860
Blair, Geo. Washington ....A. Mar. 4, 1864
*Bostwick, J. D...........................A. Sept. 2, 1864
*Black, George ....A. Dec. 1, 1865
*Bagge, Christian ....Dec. 15, 1865
*Bruguiere, Louis Gustave. ....Dec. 23, 1865
*Block, Emanuel Daniel....................A. April 6, 1866
*Bagley, William Patrick..................Nov. 24, 1868
*Beal, Rufus Jr...........................Jan. 15, 1869
*Baldwin, David Martin ....May 17, 1869
*Brooks, James Marcus ....June 25, 1869
*Barnhisel, Charles Franklin..............A. Jan. 3, 1870

*Burnham, Andrew Willard....................June 11, 1870
 Bates, Charles David.........................Sept. 30, 1870
*Baber, Andrew Jackson............ .... A. Jan. 6, 1871
*Bowen, William Jones............. ....June 23, 1871
*Brown, Rosewell Jackson..... ....A. Nov. 3, 1871
*Blake, John Joseph........ ....Mar. 22, 1872
*Balmforth, Ralph.... ....A. May 3, 1872
*Blake, George Franklin............. ... ... Feb. 21, 1873
*Barnett, Rufus Putnam....................A. Mar. 7, 1873
*Burner, John Davies.............. ... .Aug. 15 1873
*Bastian, Fritz........... ....Oct. 10, 1873
*Bankhead, Hugh...........................April 24, 1874
*Bennison, George Edward ....Aug. 28, 1874
*Bolten, William..... .... A. Nov. 6, 1874
*Buchanan, Alexander................... ....Aug. 13, 1875
 Baker, Peter ... .April 21, 1876
*Brown, Brainard Charles...... .... .June 16, 1876
*Beeby, Robert John............... .... A. Aug 3, 1877
 Brooks, Frank Howard. ....A. Jan. 4, 1878
 Brown, Orson Dana.......................A. Dec. 6, 1878
 Broad, Charles Augustus... ....A. April 4, 1879
 Bishop, Amasa Wright ....A. Sept. 5, 1879
*Bryan, Marshal Ney............... ... . .A. Sept. 2, 1881
 Bruenn, Adolph ....A. Feb. 6, 1885
 Bush, Harry Charles............. ....Dec. 2 1886
 Blood, William Frank..................... June 24, 1887
 Bowen, Thomas William..... ....A. Nov. 4, 1887
*Barnard, Ezra ....A. Feb. 1, 1889
*Berry, Fred "T"............................A. Mar. 1, 1889
 Bennett, Robert Howard.............. ... .Jan. 30, 1891
 Bullock, Richard Steele...........A. Feb. 6, 1891
 Baab, Charles........ ....May 15, 1891
 Beckwith, John Allison................. ....A. July 3, 1891
 Buteau, Samuel Hawkins ....Oct. 28, 1892
 Baumgartner, Andrew Fred................A. Aug. 4, 1893
 Baldwin, Robert Oliver ....July 20, 1894

 Chappellet, Felix............. .... Nov. 30, 1860
*Carrick, John Willard.............. ....A. Dec. 1, 1865
*Cordes, Paul Henry..................... . Dec. 22, 1865

*Chapman, "L. G."....... .... A. Nov. 2, 1866
*Crane, William Watrous........ ....May 24, 1867
*Caddy, John...... .... Nov. 27, 1868
*Chenhall, Nicholas...... ....June 18, 1869
*Cooms, Henry .... Nov. 26, 1869
Carleton; George Henry .... June 13, 1870
*Campbell, Peter..... .... Aug. 26, 1870
Clayton, William Burt........ ......Dec. 30, 1870
*Coursen, Edgar Abraham............... A. Mar. 3, 1871
*Chamberlain, Alfred Mellen. ....June 30, 1871
*Chalmers, Robert...... ....Nov. 17, 1871
*Conley, Charles..... .. .. A. Dec. 1, 1871
*Cameron, Duncan...... ....Jan 12, 1872
*Case, Isham................... .... Aug. 16, 1872
Clark, Marion ....A. Oct. 4, 1872
*Cunningham, Patrick James............ ......May 30, 1873
*Collins, William..... ....Sept. 17, 1875
*Cochran, Jesse Franklin ....A. Aug. 4, 1876
*Coburn, Thomas Cavanaugh ....July 12, 1878
*Chabot, Antone..... ....A. July 4, 1879
*Camp, Max...... ....April 30, 1880
Christy, Charles..................... .... .May 28, 1880
Cramer, Adolph Edward Henry...... .... .April 8, 1881
Colvin, Charles Lewis......... ... .July. 8, 1881
*Chandler, Edward Loomis.....................Oct. 20, 1882
Craig, Homer Alexander.... ....Sept. 25, 1885
*Cool, Geo. Washington ....Oct. 15, 1886
*Cattrell, Joseph Edward ... .Oct. 22, 1886
*Cahn, Samuel ....A. April 1, 1887
Craft, Richard Corson ....A. Feb. 3, 1888
Cassidy, Richard....... ....A. June 1, 1888
Cron, William, Jr.. ....Aug. 31, 1888
Crane, Carlton Cyrus........ ....Mar. 15, 1889
Crosman, Cortland David........ ......A. Mar. 7, 1890
*Cornall, Peter Morris......................A. Nov. 7, 1890
Cook, William Coleman ....A. Nov. 7, 1890
Culver, William Lee ....A. July 3, 1891
Capwell, Harris Cebert...... ....A. Nov. 6, 1891
Carr, Nelson........... .. .. A. Feb. 5, 1892
Champion, Albert "C."............. ....A. June 1, 1894

Chesnut, John Augustus.................. ....June 15, 1894

*Davis, James P. M. ....Aug. 19, 1854
*Dieves, Joseph, Sr.......... .... Sept. 10, 1858
*Davis, Richard A. ....Oct. 19, 1864
*D'Auteuil, George............................April 9, 1869
*Dinsmore, Luther.................... A. Dec. 6, 1872
*De Golia Darwin .... A. Sept. 1, 1876
Dalton, Henry Philip .... Sept. 22, 1882
*Dean, Samuel Case ... .April 27, 1883
*Dargie, John...... ....A. Jan. 4, 1884
Dalton, Frank Norris... ....Oct. 16, 1885
Dargie, William Edward...................... May 21, 1886
Draper, Thomas B............. ....June 26, 1891
Dalton, Henry Norris.....................A. Mar. 4, 1892
Du Bois, Elijah..... .... Jan. 19, 1894

*Evans, Morris.. ....Sept. 7, 1855
*Edmondson, P. E. ....Sept. 21, 1855
*Evans, C. W...... ....Jan. 4, 1856
Evers, John Henry........ .. .. July 26, 1867
*Estrada, Frederick ....Sept. 9, 1867
Eaton, Henry Jones ....Oct. 7, 1867
*Elliot, Matthew..... ....A.Jan. 7, 1870
Eastman, Moses Hayden.................... A. Oct. 7, 1870
*Everett, Daniel Henry. ....Jan. 19, 1877
Euson, James Henry ... .April 11, 1884
Eby, John Douglas.......................April 29, 1887
Ely, Ralph Asahel..... ....A. Jan. 3, 1895
Edoff, James "P."........ ....April 29, 1892

*Fallon, Malachi... ....A. Aug. 19, 1854
*Fish, William H............. ....Sept. 10, 1858
Farrington, Elvin Dunn.....................May 24, 1872
*Fairchild, Oscar Llewellyn Crandall.......A. July 5, 1872
*Fehr, John Lewis ....Aug. 30, 1872
*Farwell, George Elliott...... .... Nov. 29, 1872
*Francis Samuel...... ....A. Mar. 7, 1879
Furniss, Herbert Olmsted .... A. Jan. 1, 1886
Fletcher, Francis Alden...................May 16, 1890
Fisher, Charles Morrison ....July 31, 1891
Fisher, Philip Melanchton ....A. June 3, 1892

*Gieschen, John .... Dec. 24, 1861
*Gunn, John Cristar...................... A. June 2, 1865
 Gleason, George ....July 1, 1867
*Gabb, William Moore................... Nov. 25, 1867
*Gordon, Joseph S. G. ....April 17, 1868
*Graham John P..... ....June 19, 1868
*Glass, Charles ....A. Mar. 5, 1869
*Gibbons, William Peters, ...April 29, 1870
*Grosso, Constantine.... .... Feb. 23, 1872
 Gray, Martin Luther.............. ....A. May 2, 1872
 Gross, Wilhelm Gustave Constantine....... May 27, 1872
*Gemmell, Alexander ....April 19, 1872
*Gerry, Thomas.................. ....October 24, 1873
 Gardiner, James Todd ....Mar. 20, 1874
 Glascock, John Ragland ....July 9, 1875
 Gruen, John "C" ....A. Feb. 4, 1876
 Goodman, George ....A. Oct. 3, 1879
*Greenwald, Frank Julius.... ....A. Sept. 3, 1880
 Grunebaum, William Bernard...... ....July 27, 1883
 Goodfellow, George Emery............. .... June 24, 1885
*Gove, Henry Morris........... .... June 26, 1885
 Gelder, John .... A. April 6, 1888
 Glenn, John Quinn.................... July 26, 1889
 Gaskill, Varney William .... Sept. 27, 1889
 Glenn, Alexander Glenn...................Nov. 15, 1889
 Gelder, David.................................. Dec. 11, 1891
 Gardiner, William........ ....A. Oct 7, 1892

*Hayes, Patrick.......................A. Aug. 19, 1854
*Higley, Horace A.................... .....Oct. 22, 1854
*Hurtzell, Lawrence........... ....A. July 6, 1855
*Hirshberg, Samuel .... April 29, 1858
*Heymann, Reuben .. .. Jan. 14, 1859
*Hoag, Joseph W....... .... July 8, 1859
*Houghton, Frederick T..... .. ..Aug. 12, 1859
*Hillebrand William ....A. Dec. 2, 1859
*Hempel, Henry............................Mar 8, 1861
*Hagy, Adam ....A. Sept. 6, 1861
*Hodgson, Francis D .... A. Oct. 3, 1861
 Haelke Helwig Leopold...... ....A. Aug. 7, 1863
*Hise, John S. ....Mar. 23, 1864

*Howe, Micha Mead .... Dec. 2, 1864
*Hawkett, Arthur Wellington .... June 30, 1865
*Hitchcock, Harry Elisha ....A. Mar. 5, 1868
*Hobbs, Levitt Moses................... . A. Sept. 4, 1868
*Henninger, Frederick ....A. Mar. 5, 1869
*Halley, John Charles..... ....July 19, 1869
*Hartwig, Theodore .... A. Nov. 4, 1870
*Haines, Rufus Rowe..............A. June 2, 1871
*Heywood, Samuel...... .... Mar. 27, 1872
*Haas, Bernhard................. ....Sept. 20, 1872
Harlow, William Sturtevant.......... ....Mar 14, 1873
Hall, Joseph Lee........ .... Nov. 28, 1873
*Hill, William Henry ....A. Jan. 2, 1874
*Harrison, William Greer ....April 13, 1877
*Hard, Roswell Butler............ ....A. Jan. 3, 1879
*Hershberg, Leon.......................... . ....Feb. 27, 1880
*Hall, Frank Bonacina............. ....Aug. 25, 1882
Hyde, Marcus Darius ....Nov. 23, 1883
*Hallahan, Andrew ....Feb. 29, 1884
Hamilton, Noble ....A. July 4, 1884
*Hersey, Edgar Amos . ...Jan. 23, 1885
*Hammond, William Hall ....Dec. 19, 1885
Hayes, Daniel David........... ....A. Mar. 5, 1886
Haven, Charles Edward....... ....Dec. 10, 1886
Hardwick, Edward Newcomb ....Jan. 28, 1887
Hyde, Clarence ....April 22, 1887
*Handy, Brayton Everington ....A. Sept 7, 1888
Hewitt, Robert Ethelbert ....Aug. 30, 1889
Haven, Clarence.................. ....Oct. 18, 1889
Holland, Arthur Percy ....Feb. 14, 1890
Hooe, Headley Smith.......... ....Mar. 28, 1890
*Hall, Robert James ....A. June 6, 1890
Harmon, Dana................. ....A. Feb. 6, 1891
Hoppen, Alfred ....Feb. 7, 1891
Humphrey, Thomas Marshall ....A. Mar. 6, 1891
Hall, Edward Masser, Jr .... June 12, 1891
Hart, Edward Henry..... .... Aug. 21, 1891
Hunt, Henry Osgood.......... ....A. Mar. 4, 1892
*Hammon, Wendell Philucius. ....A. April 1, 1892
Hough, George Walles...... ....A. Dec. 2, 1892

Hatfield, William Richy......................A. Mar. 3, 1893

*Irwin, William H...........................Aug. 16, 1868
Irwin, John Clarke........................ May 27, 1872
*Irish, John Powell........ ....Nov. 26, 1886

*Jones, Benjamin Lovie....... ....Aug. 19, 1854
*Justice, Patterson C................. ......Aug 5, 1859
*Johnson, Perry.............................June 1, 1860
*Jahn, Henry................................Dec. 24, 1861
*Janssen, Frederick George Ernest......... ......Oct. 27, 1869
*Jose, William Hacking ....May 8, 1874
*Jensen, Rasmus..... ....Feb. 19, 1875
Joyce, Austin Ambrose.................. ......Sept 23, 1887

*Kellersberger, J ....Mar. 9, 1855
Kyte, James Carter.................. ....Nov. 3, 1859
*Knawer, Frederick...........................A. July 5, 1867
*Kennedy, William.......... .... A. May 2, 1873
*Kindgren, Christian Wilhelm. ....Jan. 17, 1875
*Kennedy, James..............................A. Sept. 3, 1875
*Knudson, Andrew...........................July 28, 1876
*King, William Andrew ....A. Oct. 6, 1876
*Kahn, Israel.........................A. Sept. 1, 1882
*Knapp, Charles Richard..... .... Sept. 9, 1882
Knight, Frederick Wales.....................Sept. 29, 1882
Keesing, Henry Bernard........ .... Aug. 21, 1885
Kendall, Frank Irving................. ....July 22, 1887
Kelley, Charles Marsh ....A. Nov. 4, 1887
Kerr, Archie Fullerton........................A. Aug. 4, 1893

*Lengfeld, Louis... ....A. Aug. 19, 1854
*Lacy, D. S. ....Jan. 21, 1855
*Linden, Henry........ ....April 29, 1858
Lentell, James........ ....Jan. 21, 1859
*Lathrop, H. P..................... ....March 25, 1859
*Lutger, Gustavus................................March 9, 1863
*Leinhoop, Frederick........... .. ,...........April 15, 1864
*Laing, John ....Nov. 2, 1864
*Little, John ....Aug. 11, 1871
Luelling, Oregon "C".......................April 30, 1875

*Lindeman, Henry.................... ....A. Aug. 4, 1876
*Lamont, Thomas ....Aug. 11, 1876
*Logan, Oliver Cunningham..................A. April 2, 1880
Lamoureux, Philias Henry...... ....Aug. 26, 1881
Lebrecht, William...... ....April 27, 1883
*Levy, Meyer Samuel.................May 25, 1883
*Lilliencrantz, August... ....A. Oct. 1, 1886
Lanyon, Joseph Henry...................A. May 3, 1889
Leber, Albert Lewis................... June 28, 1889
Lawrence, Henry Hathaway, Jr. ....Feb. 21, 1890
Lord, Leslie Howard................ ....June 30, 1893
Lindsay, Thomas ....A. Oct. 6, 1893

*McKee, Samuel Bell........... ....Oct. 22, 1854
*McDevitt, A. D.................March 30, 1855
*Myers, A. H....................A. July 6, 1860
Miner, James Ogden ....Sept. 7, 1860
*Mead, James Flendrowe.. .... Nov. 23, 1867
*Merritt, Frederick A..................... ..... April 21, 1868
*Massey, Benjamin Franklin. ....May 28, 1869
*Maloon, Benjamin........ .... Aug. 20, 1869
*Mann, Benjamin Franklin...................Aug 30, 1869
*Marshall, William Board................A. Oct. 7, 1870
*McKeever, Charles........ ....A. Dec. 2, 1870
*McKenzie, William William ....Aug. 25, 1871
*Matthews, Julius Case ....A. June 7, 1872
*McConnel, James Davisen............... A. June 7, 1872
*Marsh, Charles Pantier ....A. Sept. 6, 1872
Marsh, John Carlton............. ....April 11, 1873
Martin, James Christopher.... ....A. Nov. 7, 1873
*Mason, Joseph Robinson........ ....A. Jan. 2, 1874
*McCord, William "P" .... A. Nov. 6, 1874
*McKeen, Albert Atwater............. ... .Feb. 26, 1875
*McGregor, John.... ....Mar. 12, 1875
*McKee, Robert Linington...... ....Nov. 24, 1876
*McClure, Stewart ....Mar. 22, 1878
*Mattingly, John Andrew........ ....Mar. 21, 1879
*Maass, Aug. Nicolias William ....May 21, 1880
*Moore, John Solon.................... ....A. Feb. 4, 1881
*Moore, Theodore Staunton............. ....A. June 3, 1881

Morrison, John..... ....June 17, 1881
*Murphy, John Henry........ ....A. Sept. 2, 1881
Matthews, Francis Ima ... .Oct. 12, 1883
*Murphy, William Leander.................A. Sept. 7, 1883
Mayer, Leopold... .... A. Jan. 4, 1884
*Mothersole, George John........ ....A. Aug. 1, 1884
*Merritt, Ambrose......................... ...... Sept. 19, 1884
Mueller, Herman Emanuel........ ....May 29, 1885
McCarron, David.................. .... Nov. 19, 1886
Mauzy, Byron .... Nov. 11, 1887
McMullen, David Alexander................. Feb. 17, 1888
Momyer, Henry Eastman .... A. Nov. 2, 1888
McPike, Henry Clay........ ....Feb. 15, 1889
Metcalf, Victor Howard...... .... Sept. 13, 1889
McMullen, John C....... ....A. Jan. 3, 1890
Man, Charles Frederick ....Mar. 14, 1890
Morris, Benjamin Samuel ....May 23, 1890
McPherson, Alexander Lewis......... ....Aug. 8, 1890
McKenzie, William .... A. Jan. 2, 1891
McCarter, John....... ....A. Nov 6, 1891
Morris, William ....A. Jan. 1, 1892
Manuel, Walter Griswold................. ..May 20, 1892

*Nolan, Stephen.... ... .August 28, 1863
*Nicholson, Isaac Earnest .... A. Sept. 3, 1869
*Nielsen, Anders Peter William ....June 12, 1871
Naismith, George Semple .... A. June 4, 1880
Nordhausen, Charles Christian ....A. June 4, 1880
Nordhausen, Ernest Albert ....Aug. 20, 1880
Northey, Vernal Sidney........ ....A. May 7, 1886
Nelson, James Wesley..........................Sept. 11, 1891
Newsom, Joseph Cather.......................Nov. 27, 1891

*Owen, L. C....... ....A. Aug. 19, 1854
*Oltman, William ....…Sept. 6, 1869
*Oakes, Daniel Briggs... ....Feb. 9, 1872
*Owens, John....... ....July 18, 1873
*Olmsted, Sheldon Patterson........... ... A. Mar. 3, 1876
Outram, David John... .... June 17, 1881
*Osborne, Orlando Canning.....................July 8, 1881

Otto, Frederick G.......................................A. May 1. 1885
Oyler, Robert...A. Feb. 5. 1887
Owen, Wm. Henry Searles.......................April 24. 1891
Ogden, Frank Burroughs..........................Sept. 28. 1894

*Paddock, Isaac E......................................A. Aug. 19. 1854
*Parker, Marvel..Jan 21. 1855
*Paul, Colin..A. Aug. 3. 1860
*Pinkerton, Thomas Hamil........................A. July 5. 1867
*Prosser, Walter ....A. Feb. 7. 1868
*Pratt, Daniel Webster...............................June 12. 1868
*Partenscky, Charles.................................March 26. 1869
*Pfiester, Julius ....A. Sept. 3. 1869
*Palmer, Smith..Oct. 8. 1869
*Palmer, George McKenzie........................Nov. 29. 1869
*Patterson, William James.........................June 9. 1871
*Pomroy, Horace Barton ....A. Aug. 2. 1872
*Phelan, William Seymour.........................A. Dec. 6. 1872
*Powers, Oliver Pollard.............................A. Sept. 4. 1874
*Pierce, John Hiram ....Nov. 19. 1880
*Plunkett, James California........................June 10. 1881
*Perry, William Francis.............................July 29. 1881
*Patterson, John Whiteley.........................A. Sept. 2. 1881
Pierce, Charles Dexter...............................Sept. 9. 1881
Parrish, William Henry ....June 8. 1883
Patterson, Albert Lewis Crandall..............A. May 1. 1885
*Peck, John Amma ....Aug. 27. 1886
Price, Wallace Covert................................July 8. 1887
*Perry, Arthur Miley................................A. Dec. 2. 1887
Parrish, Norman Adolph ....Jan. 20. 1893

*Robinson, Samuel Hayward......................A. Aug. 19. 1854
*Richards, William....................................A. Feb. 4. 1856
*Robertson, James A..................................Nov. 12. 1860
Reinstadler, Francois.................................A. Dec. 5. 1862
*Ross, John ....April 28. 1865
*Read, W. D..A. Dec. 1. 1865
*Rector, Ludwell James..............................Nov. 9. 1867
*Reyburn, Thomas Samuel.........................May 16. 1869
*Reid, Charles Wood.................................Mar. 25. 1870

*Reynolds, John Newton................ ....Sept. 9, 1870
Rosenberg, Morris... .... April 21, 1871
*Robertson, Daniel......... .... A. June 7, 1872
Russell, Edward Knight.............. .... A. July 5, 1872
*Richardson, Aaron Sandborn . ... A. Dec. 6, 1872
Roff, Harry Loren.. ....Jan. 24, 1873
*Ruth, John........................ ....April 18, 1873
Rasmussen, Haus ....Feb. 12, 1875
*Ryttenberg, Isaac David...................A. Aug. 3, 1877
Reichling, Louis Frank.......... .... July 30, 1880
Robinson, Edward Constant.. ....July 22, 1881
*Richardson, Charles................ ....A. July 1, 1887
Richards, John Callahan........... ....A. Oct. 4, 1889
*Reckard, Edward Lockwood..................Mar. 30, 1891
Rogers, Josiah Barnes.............. .... June 16, 1893
Reinhardt, Joseph.................... ....Oct. 27, 1893
Revalk, Richmond Emil...... ....A. Dec. 1, 1893
Rabe, John........ ....A Nov. 2, 1894

*Spicer, H. C....... ....A. Aug. 19, 1854
Shattuck, Francis Kittridge...... .. .. Nov. 4, 1854
*Scott, John............. ....April 27, 1855
*Stratton, James T............ ....Feb. 11, 1859
*Smith, E. J ... .A. Nov. 3, 1865
*Skinner, Chester Clark. ....July 13, 1866
*Smith, George Frank....... . ... May 31, 1867
Schmidt, John Carl........ ....Oct. 11, 1867
*Smith, Joseph....... .... A. Dec. 6, 1867
*Scott, John Vance.................... ....Dec. 8, 1868
*Schneider, C. P.. ....A. Feb. 7, 1868
*Sidden, James................. . ... Jan. 11, 1869
*Stone, Winfield Scott... ....April 19, 1869
*Slicer, Hugh....... ... . .Sept. 3, 1869
*Spraul, Alonzo Thompson.................A. Oct. 1, 1869
*Simpson, Real Benjamin...... . ...A. May 6, 1870
*Stevens, Francis . ...A. July 1, 1870
*Snyder, Lyman Nutt........... .... June 14, 1872
*Striker, John Wesley.... ....A. Dec. 6, 1872
*Schoffner, Friedrick ....A. March 7, 1873
Snyder, Andrew Jackson.............. ....A. Aug. 1, 1873

Simpson, Joseph Cairn.................. ....A. March 5. 1875
*Stahl, Benjamin Franklin............ ......A. June 4. 1875
Schaffer, Louis (No. 1)......................Jan. 17, 1879
*Strathern, William... ....April 11, 1879
Schaffer, Louis (No. 2)... .... Oct. 27, 1882
Smilie, Robert ....Nov. 17. 1882
Schuller, Antonio........... .. .. A. April 6, 1883
*Share, Alfred Joseph .... ..June 29, 1883
Sutherland, Edwin ....A. July 4. 1884
Spiars, Frank William .. .. Oct 30, 1885
Samson, Martin Meyer...... .... A. Nov. 6, 1885
*Steele, Spear Spencer......................Mar. 25. 1887
Schlarbaum, John Christian Benedict...A. March 4. 1887
Steffanoni, Achilles........... ....April 12, 1887
*Stewart, Michael Young.....................A. July 1, 1887
Stampley, Orville Knighton.................A. July 1, 1887
*Stephenson, John Calvin.................. ..Sept. 15, 1887
*Snell, Richard Bailey....... ....Dec. 23, 1887
Samuels, Isaac Julius........... .... Aug. 17, 1888
Smoot, David Lowe .... A. Dec. 7, 1888
Smith, Benjamin John ....Jan. 25, 1889
Swain, Clinton Terry. .... Feb. 22, 1889
Sweeney, George Wade .... A. April 5, 1889
Stimpson, George Washington........... A. June 7, 1889
Schlesinger, Adolph Charles... .... July 19, 1889
*Southard, William Freeman .... A. Sept. 6, 1889
Slemin, Charles, Jr................... ...... A. July 3, 1891
Samuels, Julius...... .... A. July 3, 1891
*Smith, Henry Talbot...... ....Oct 9, 1891
Seaton, Horace Scott............... . ...June 17, 1892
Schulze, Max Charles ....Sept. 23, 1892
Shakespeare, James ....April 28, 1893

*Ticknor, Daniel...... .... .Mar. 30, 1860
Taylor, James.. ....A. Dec. 4, 1863
*Todtmann, Theodore Ernst..... ....July 26, 1872
*Tirrill, Layfayette...... ....A. Mar. 7, 1873
*Tilley, Gabriel Henderson............... A. Nov. 3, 1876
Troy, John Henry. ....A. July 4. 1879
*Tillotson, Henry Ira.................. ....Feb. 25, 1881

Thomson, Arthur Dalliba ....Mar. 26, 1886
Thompson, Frank Robert........ ....May 11, 1888
Taylor, Charles Benjamin. ....A. May 3, 1889
Taylor, Felton ....A. May 2, 1890
Turner, Joshua Nichols ... .Oct. 31, 1890
Trenschel, August Frederick............. ... April 15, 1892
*Thomson, Stuart Coventry........... ....Aug. 19, 1892
Tozer, Charles Francis.................... ..... July 28, 1893
Tillson, Fred Minot .... Sept. 14, 1894
Trotter, John.. ....Nov. 30, 1694

Umphred, Frank Morris ....A. Feb. 7, 1890
Umphred, Joseph Wilson ....A. Feb. 6, 1891

*Van Voorhies, William..... ....A. March 4, 1859
*Vogt, David........... ... . Jan. 22, 1869
Veitch, William Thomas............... ....Sept. 16, 1881

*Whitcher, Jeremiah Elkins............. .A. Aug. 19, 1854
Warner, Franklin..................... ......A. Dec. 2, 1854
*Willis, E. J....... ....A. Sept. 7, 1855
*Williams, Alpheus Fuller... .... A. Mar. 4, 1864
*Wellendorf, Louis........... .... A. Feb. 3, 1865
*Willes, D. Ellis....... ....A. Feb. 3, 1866
*Walker, Lysander..... ....A. Jan. 4, 1867
*Webster, Johnathan Vinson.................. July 30, 1869
*Ward, Robert...... .... April 4, 1868
*Wales, Thatcher Peter........... .... A. Sept. 6, 1868
*Wallis, Albert........................ ....Mar. 11, 1870
*Watson, William Callaghan.......... .....A. Nov. 3, 1871
*Watkins, Henry Percival.......... ...... A. Aug. 2, 1872
Wilson, James ....Mar. 21, 1873
Woolsey, Elliott Hartman .... A. Nov. 7, 1873
*Williams, Mark Anthony ....June 26, 1874
Williams, Nicholas.... ....Mar. 24, 1876
*Wright, Edward Lawrence ....Feb. 21, 1879
*Wonderlich, John Peter .... A. April 4, 1879
*Wright, Williard Carroll ....Oct. 24, 1879
*Wallace, George ....May 22, 1885
*Weyhe, Charles Henry....................A. June 5, 1885

Westover, Clinton......   Nov. 18. 1887
Warner, Junia Josiah...........   ...... Feb. 8. 1889
*Wallace, Louis Burton......   ......June 13. 1890
Wines, Charles Latham ....Oct. 16. 1890
Wines, Charles Buckley   ... .A. Dec. 5. 1890
Wheeler, Roscoe, Jr ....Jan. 29. 1892
Wundsch, Joseph ....June 24. 1892
Wilkinson, Edward Melville   May 19. 1893
Woods, William Fowler........   ......Sept. 30. 1893

*Yard, George Malcomson ....A. Aug. 19. 1854

Zabel, Julius.....................   ..A. Nov. 7. 1868

* Not now members

A. Affiliated.

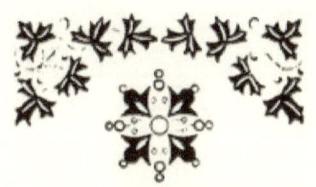

www.ingramcontent.com/pod-product-compliance
Lightning Source LLC
Chambersburg PA
CBHW032204010726
47493CB00008BA/2822